KU-438-396

Squeaky Cleaners

in a muddle!

Vivian French

illustrated by

Anna Currey

Hodder
Children's
Books

00223

a division of Hodder Headline plc

MILNATHORT PRIMARY SCHOOL

To my nephews
Anna Currey

Text copyright © Vivian French 1996
Illustration copyright © Anna Currey 1996

This edition published as a My First Read Alone
in 1998 by Hodder Children's Books

The right of Vivian French and Anna Currey to be
identified as the Author and Illustrator of the Work has
been asserted by them in accordance with the Copyright,
Designs and Patents Act 1988.

10   9   8   7   6   5   4   3   2

All rights reserved. No part of this publication may be
reproduced, stored in a retrieval system, or transmitted,
in any form or by any means without the prior written
permission of the publisher, nor be otherwise circulated
in any form of binding or cover other than that in which
it is published and without a similar condition being
imposed on the subsequent purchaser.

ISBN 0 340 72665 2

Printed and bound in Great Britain
by The Devonshire Press, Torquay, TQ2 7NX

Hodder Children's Books
a Division of Hodder Headline plc
338 Euston Road
London NW1 3BH

One

'Hi Nina! Hi Gina! There's a wonderful view from here!'

Nina and Gina looked up and saw Fred balancing his way along the ridge of the roof.

'I'm going to sweep the chimney!'
he called down. 'I thought the Squeaky
Cleaners might offer a new service!'

'Oh dearie dearie me!' Gina went
pale. 'I could never climb a chimney!
Oh, dear Fred – don't even think of it!'

Nina snorted. 'Don't take any notice,
Gina. The Squeaky Cleaners are house
cleaners – not chimney sweeps.'
'BRRRINGGGGGGGG!'
The telephone rang.

'I'll get it,' said Nina, hurrying indoors.

Gina stayed outside. She watched anxiously as Fred pushed a brush into the chimney. There was a sudden flurry of soot, and a squeak from Fred.

'Fred! Fred! Are you all right?' Gina hopped up and down in agitation.

Fred peered down, his eyes very bright in his blackened face.

'Fine! But I dropped the brush!'

The front door opened and Nina appeared. She was covered in soot smuts.

'FRED!' she shouted.

'Oops,' said
Fred, and slid
down the ladder.

'The house
is filthy!' Nina said
crossly. 'And we won't
have time to clean up
because we've got to go out. That was
Mrs Bird on the phone – she needs our
help this minute!'

'A bird?' Gina said. 'Does that mean we've got to clean a nest?'

'That's right,' said Nina. 'And we're going at once! Well – as soon as I've cleaned myself up.'

Two

Mrs Bird fluttered from branch to
branch, hanging out washing. Behind
her, six little baby birds, all clean and
brushed, cheeped and squabbled.

'Do be good, my little tweetie pies,'
Mrs Bird told them with her beak full of
clothes pegs. 'Grandmother is coming to
stay and we must be tidy!'

'Mother!' shrieked
the biggest baby.
'Charlie
pushed me!'

'Didn't!' shouted Charlie, and he jumped up and flapped his wings. The pile of clean wet washing slipped off the edge of the nest and fell in a muddy puddle below with a huge SPLASH!

Mrs Bird squawked loudly and dropped all the pegs.

Fred roared up on his motorbike.
BRRRRRRRRRRRRMMMMMMM!

Chugga chugga chugga chugga chug!
Nina and Gina drove up behind
Fred in their van. Gina held tightly to her
basket of dusters and looked worried.

'Gina, don't worry!' Nina said as she put on the brakes. 'A nest box is no different from anyone else's house – it's just up in a tree!'

'Eeeek!' Gina said in a feeble voice.

Nina shook her head and climbed out of the van. Gina followed her, trembling. Fred hurried over to unload the ladder from the van roof.

'Here we go!' he said, and swung the ladder against the tree.

Mrs Bird flapped down to the ground.

'So kind of you to come,' she said.
'Grandmother Bird is coming to stay,
and my dear little babies are such a
handful. I can't make the nest look tidy
whatever I do . . . and now all the
washing has fallen in a puddle!'

Gina put down her basket with a thump. 'Don't you worry,' she said. 'We'll sort it out. Fred will look after the babies, and Nina and I will clean your nest from top to bottom. And we'll see to the washing. You fly along and meet Grandmother Bird.'

Mrs Bird fluffed out her feathers. 'Oh, how wonderful you are,' she smiled.

'I'll be off. Back soon, my birdie babies!'

21

With a flip and a flap of her wings, she was off over the trees and flying into the distance.

Fred and Nina stared at Gina.

'Gina!' Nina said. 'Whatever came over you?'

Gina tied her apron a little tighter.
'Well,' she said, 'I do hate a muddle.
And that Mrs Bird isn't going to be
much help here,
is she?'

She skipped
up the ladder
and into
the nest.

Fred looked at Nina. 'Whistling
whiskers!'

'Exactly,' Nina said. 'I'd better help
her. And you'd better take all those
babies somewhere to play!'

Fred twirled his tail. 'You mean I don't have to do any cleaning? Just play with a few babies?'

Nina nodded. 'I'll send them down the ladder. They can't fly yet. Just don't let them get dirty before their grandmother arrives.'

'Easy!' said Fred.

Three

'La la la la!' Gina sang. She was up to
her elbows in soap and suds. Beside
her Nina was sorting out a huge pile
of rubbish.

'There's nothing as good as a nice clean house!' Gina said as she scrubbed and scrubbed at the grubby and grimy floor.

'That's right,' Nina said. She leant on her broom for a moment. 'I wonder how Fred's getting on?'

'Those dear little babies!' Gina said.
'I expect he's having a lovely time.'

Fred wasn't.

'Mr Mouse! Mr Mouse! Can we ride on your motorbike?' Charlie asked.

'No,' said Fred.

'But we want to!' said Charlie, and he half fluttered and half scrambled on to the handlebars.

'Us too! Us too!' said the other baby birds.

'GET DOWN THIS MINUTE!' Fred said crossly.

'Shan't!' said the biggest baby.

'Shan't!' said all the others.

Fred scratched his head. The baby
birds looked so sweet and fluffy . . .
except for their eyes. Their eyes were
bright and beady and very determined.

Fred coughed. 'If you get down,' he
said, 'I'll give you a special treat!'

There was a fluttering and flapping and the babies stood in a row gazing at Fred, expectantly.

'Um,' said Fred, and coughed again. His mind was racing. What on earth was a special treat for six little baby birds?

'Um,' he said slowly, 'we're going to play . . . ring a ring a roses.'

There was a short silence.

'YAAAAAAAAAAAAAAAAHHHHH!' shrieked the baby birds.

'That's not special,' said the littlest.

'That's for babies!' said Charlie.

'Let's get back on the bike!' said another baby.

'NO!'
yelled Fred.

'Then we'll jump in the dirty puddle
with Mother's washing!' said Charlie.

Fred watched in horror as all six baby birds jumped in the puddle with a muddy SPLOSHHHHHH!

'That was special,' said the littlest. 'That was nice! Let's do it again!' And they did.

Four

Up in the nest box Gina looked round
in approval. 'It's beginning to look
much better,' she said. 'One last polish
and shine and we'll be finished.'

Nina nodded. 'I'll pop down and fetch the dirty washing,' she said.

'We might even have time to play with those sweet little babies!' Gina said as Nina disappeared down the ladder.

The sweet little babies were taking it
in turns to splatter each other with
muddy water. Their feathers were clotted
with dirt, and only their eyes were
shining. Fred sat on the grass beside
them.

'They can't get any dirtier,' he thought to himself, 'so they may as well stay here. But whatever will Nina and Gina say?' He sighed and glanced up at the nest. To his horror he saw Nina swinging herself on to the ladder.

'PSSSSSSSSST!' Fred hissed.

The babies stared at him.

'Quick!' Fred whispered. He
scampered away and hid under
the bushes.

The babies
scurried after him,
wondering what he
was up to.

Nina reached the bottom of the
ladder and looked at the washing.

It was heaped at the edge of the puddle.

She dropped it into a bucket with a squelch and climbed slowly back with the bucket on her shoulder. It was very heavy.

'Oi, Mr Mouse!' the littlest bird said in a loud voice. 'I want to go back to the puddle!'

Fred didn't answer. He was listening.
There was the faint sound of bubbling
water. He tiptoed through the bushes.

A stream! A small, clear, silvery
stream trickling between two rocks!

'Babies!' called Fred. 'Here is your special treat. You can all jump in!'

The baby birds didn't move. Clean water was much too much like washing.

'Look!' Fred said desperately. 'It's fun!' And he jumped in himself.

BRRRRRRRRRR! The water was freezing cold. Fred's teeth chattered and he trembled all over.

'I'll never ever ever get out of cleaning houses again,' he said to himself. Not *ever*!

Out loud he said, 'You can splash me if you like!'

SPLASHHHHHHHHH!

Six baby birds arrived on top of Fred. They splashed and they sploshed and they rolled him over and over in the water.

At last Fred could see that they were as clean as clean could be. He took a deep breath. 'Everybody back to the bike!'

There was a massive rush. Fred, dripping, trailed behind. By the time he reached his bike all six babies were on board.

'At least they're clean,' he thought.
'All I need to do now is dry them . . .
I know!'

FIVE

Mrs Bird and Grandmother Bird flew
over the trees towards Mrs Bird's nest.

'I do hope your home is tidy, dear,'
said Grandmother. 'Last time I came it
was a shocking mess!'

Mrs Bird gave a little laugh. 'Oh, Mother! Of course it's tidy!'

The two of them swooped downwards.

'Well!' said Grandmother Bird, 'I am
surprised!'

Mrs Bird's nest was gleaming with
cleanliness. Everything was shining and
as neat as neat could be.

Down below, five spotless little baby birds were lined up on the top of the van.

The sixth was riding round and round on the back of Fred's motorbike, her wings spread out wide in the sunshine. A few last drops of water sparkled on her feathers.

'Goodness me!' said
Grandmother, and she
flew down to hug her
grandchildren.

Mrs Bird hugged Nina and Gina.

'Thank you so much!' she whispered.
'And thank Fred for me! How did he
keep my babies so clean and happy?'

'They're such sweet babies,' Gina
said. 'Anyone could look after them!'
She and Nina scrambled down the
ladder.

Fred was leaning against his bike, his
eyes closed.

'Had a good day, Fred?' Nina asked.

Fred tried to stop a yawn. 'Oh yes,' he said. 'No problems.'

Nina grinned. 'Mrs Bird wondered if you'd like to look after the babies tomorrow?'

There was no answer except for the roar of a motorbike. Fred had vanished.

Six

When Nina and Gina reached home
Fred was fast asleep. The house was
gleaming.

'Oh Nina!' Gina said. 'Fred's cleaned
up the soot!'

'I think,' Nina said, 'from now on Fred may prefer cleaning to baby-sitting!'

'Nonsense!' said Gina. 'Those dear babies!'

Fred stirred. 'Dear babies?' he muttered. 'I'd rather clean all week!' And he went on snoring.